Amish Outcasts

Book — Two

The **AMISH**
Girl and her
Garden

Samantha Bayarr

Table of Contents

The Amish Girl and her Garden
Amish Outcasts: Book Two

Copyright © 2017 by Samantha Bayarr

ATTENTION READERS:

This book is a continuation from Book #1, The Amish Bishop's Disgrace. You must read Book #1 FIRST if you want the best possible reading experience.

You can find Book #1 HERE

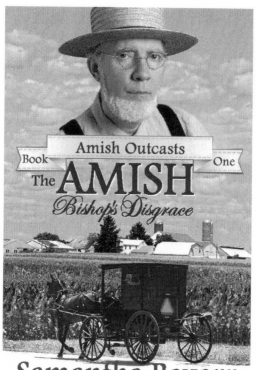

Newly Released books
always FREE with
Kindle Unlimited.
♡ LOVE to Read?
♡ LOVE Discount Books?
♡ LOVE GIVEAWAYS?

SIGN UP NOW
Click the Link Below to Join
my Exclusive Mailing List

PLEASE CLICK <u>HERE</u> to SIGN UP!

Our Father, who art in Heaven, hallowed be thy name. Thy Kingdom come, Thy will be done; on earth as it is in Heaven. Give us this day our daily bread and forgive us our sins as we forgive those who have sinned against us.
Lead us not into temptation, but deliver us from all that is evil; for Thine is the kingdom, the power and the glory forever. Amen. Matthew 6:9-13

Chapter One

Melody Fisher hummed a hymn from the *Ausbund* as she steered her horse and buggy onto the new covered bridge over Peace Creek.

Chestnut's ears twitched as his hooves clapped down on the wooden planks and he let out a snort and a low groan.

An old man in a black hat unexpectedly stepped out from the shadows at the far end of the bridge, startling Melody.

She tightened up the reins, hoping he'd move, but he seemed as if he needed help.

He was Amish—Old Order, but she'd never seen him before. He was dirty, and his clothes were tattered—as if he was homeless; was such a thing possible in their community? Since she didn't know him, she didn't want to stop, but he was blocking the path and she couldn't go around him without hitting him.

"Whoa, Boy!" Melody said to Chestnut.

As the man approached, something in his eyes made her heart speed up. His stare made her nervous, and she darted her eyes to see if there was enough room to pass around him. He was on foot and could easily jump

7

from one side to the next quickly and remain in her way. If she tried to back the horse, she'd hit the sidewall of the bridge.

Lily, her eight-year-old daughter, was at her shoulder from the back seat. "What's wrong, *Mamm?*"

"Sit back down, Lily," she said, trying to steady her shaky voice.

"Are you lost?" she called out to the old man, wondering where he'd come from since there wasn't an Old Order Amish community in the area.

He stopped near Chestnut, causing the animal to grunt and whinny, his ears twitching madly. The animal seemed to sense something was awry, and it made Melody so uneasy she could taste the stickiness of adrenaline on her tongue.

The old man narrowed his eyes. "I'm visiting *mei sohn.*"

"Where does your son live?" she asked.

He twisted up his face. "*Mei sohn* is dead!" he shouted.

Melody jumped.

She knew who he was; there were rumors in the community that the old Bishop had been let out of jail recently. But what would he be doing here at the bridge? Didn't he have an ankle bracelet on?

Her gaze traveled to his pant leg; just over his boot was a black band with two little boxes on each side of his leg, a green light blinking on one side.

"I went back to jail for another year because of you, when all I wanted to do was see *mei grandkinner*. Now I have to wear this ankle bracelet for another year!"

Melody shook her head; he had her mistaken for her cousin, Eva.

"When the police caught me at your house, they wouldn't listen to me; I only wanted to see *mei sohn's boppli,* and you wouldn't let me see her!"

Melody's breath hitched, and she lifted her gaze to meet his.

He chuckled. "I convinced them to extend *mei* boundaries to the bridge, so I could visit Adam, but I can't go beyond the bridge!" he said with a raised voice. "I've been waiting for you every day since I was set free. I told you I'd come back for you, Eva!"

Melody felt Lily at her back again, and she reached behind her to move the child back to her seat. "Eva's *mei* cousin," she said, her voice shaky.

She knew the history and the story behind this man's troubles, but she didn't look enough like Eva for him to mistake her for her cousin, did she?

"You're Eva Yoder and you killed *mei sohn!*"

Her flesh prickled as her blood ran through her veins with an icy chill.

"Nee," she cried, shaking her head. "I'm not Eva—it wasn't me!"

Melody tugged on the reins to back up the horse, but the Bishop grabbed the harness.

"You're not getting away, Eva, you're going to join Adam in the ravine."

Melody and Lily screamed.

Chestnut reared and squealed.

The Bishop waved his arms and hollered to agitate the horse, and then slapped his flank, causing him to buck.

Melody screamed, yanking on the reins and pulling back with all her might.

"Whoa!" She sobbed. "Stop it; leave me alone. I'm not Eva!"

From the back seat, Lily screamed as the open buggy jostled back and forth.

Melody convulsed with sobs as she snaked her hands around the reins hoping to control the horse. "Somebody help me!" she screamed.

The horse squealed and snorted as he lifted his front legs, causing the buggy to teeter, dumping Lily out onto the wooden floor of the bridge with a thud.

"Run, Lily, run home," Melody screamed.

Bishop Byler tightened his grip on the harnesses and shoved at the horse. He slapped his side so hard, he bolted backward about a hundred feet, slamming the buggy into the wall of the bridge. The sudden jolt threw Melody from her seat, catapulting her out the window head first. A fading scream escaped her on the way down the ravine until a small splash reverberated up from the shallow creek.

"Please help my *mamm,*" Lily begged him. "Please!"

He rushed to the window and let out a belly laugh before turning to face Lily. "No one can help her now; she's joined *mei sohn* in the afterlife," he growled at her."

Lily stood in the middle of the bridge crying for her mother, her eyes wide and fearful, but she couldn't move.

As the Bishop ambled toward her, Lily's breaths came in short bursts, propelled only by the uncontrollable sobbing that now shook her limbs. Tears slid down her cheeks and her nose dripped. She stood there not moving until the Bishop was almost too close to run from.

He took another step toward her, as if it was a game to him. Lily inched back toward the end of the bridge after he took another step. Her whole body shook, and she heaved in her breaths. The Bishop quickened his steps, closing the space between them. Her eyes locked with his and she blinked away tears.

She stumbled as her foot teetered over the threshold of the bridge into the dirt road. She fell backward, bracing herself with her hands.

The Bishop reached the edge of the bridge and bent down to grab her, but she scooted backward on her haunches. His hand caught the end of her shoe; she screamed as she wriggled out of it and scrambled backward in the dirt.

Her gaze dropped when the blinking green light on his ankle bracelet turned red. The Bishop looked down at his ankle and then stood there staring at her as he drew back his leg. The device blinked green again.

I can't go beyond the bridge, he'd told her mother.

Bishop Byler lurched forward, grabbing for her once more, catching the end of her foot, but she pulled on it and scooted back out of his reach.

He stopped and stared at her for a minute; she was still sobbing, but content that he couldn't leave the bridge; his ankle bracelet would alert the police and he'd go back to jail.

Lily watched him, fear paralyzing her.

"We'll meet again," he said with a slight chuckle. "I promise!"

She sat there in the dirt, unable to move, as she watched him walk back toward the other end of the bridge and out of sight.

Chapter Two

Lily stared with unseeing eyes while Chestnut bucked repeatedly, his whinnying muffled. The sun sparkled over Peace Creek, the reflection nearly blinding her.

Her *mamm* was down there somewhere below the bridge; she needed help, but Lily hadn't moved. How long she'd sat there was unknown to her.

Chestnut bucked again, startling her.

Her gaze lifted to the struggling animal, but she couldn't help him; she needed to help her *mudder.*

Pushing herself up from the ground, her limbs were shaky and caused her to stumble back into the dirt. She tried a second time and lost her footing again. Fresh sobs shook her tiny frame as she attempted a third time to rise to her feet, but it was no use; she was too weak and shaky.

She rose to her knees and scrambled across the dirt road into the grassy area that led down a steep embankment to the creek below.

She peered over the edge of the drop and let out a strangled cry. Her *mamm* was down there, half in the water.

"*Mamm,*" she screamed, sobs convulsing her when she didn't get a response.

Turning around, she slowly skidded down feet first, grappling the tall, grassy plants for leverage.

17

About mid-way, she looked down at her mother; panic seized her, paralyzing her momentarily.

"I can't save you, *Mamm,"* she blubbered. "I'm sorry!"

She leaned forward in the grass and pressed her face against it, hugging the steep levee of warm earth. Shifting slightly, her foot slipped on a rock, sending her tumbling down head over heels several times in between screams.

Landing upright on a ledge, she looked down at her mother; her head was spinning, and she closed her eyes to keep from vomiting. She didn't have much further to go, but it was a steep grade. Her gaze traveled to the edge of the grassy shelf where she'd landed, locating a spot where she could jump to the next ridge; it was mostly level ground from that point to where her mother lay face-up on the creek bank.

"I'm coming, *Mamm,*" Lily cried out.

Her voice echoed in the gully.

She looked up toward the bridge where she could hear Chestnut still whinnying and snorting about his displeasure with being jammed up against the side of the bridge.

She shimmied over to the end of the low rise she'd settled onto and turned back around to inch her way down the rest of the way into the ravine to rescue her mother. She shook and sobbed, which made her journey more difficult, but fear for her mother pushed her forward.

When she was close enough to see her mother clearly, she was elated to see that her eyes were open. "*Mamm,* I'm coming," she called down to her.

Picking up her pace, she slipped several times in the tall grass that was still damp from early morning dew. Her hands and knees were scraped and bloody, but she pressed on, determined to reach her mother.

"*Mamm,* I'm here," Lily said, collapsing beside her mother.

Melody winced when her daughter laid her head on her chest, and as much as she wanted Lily near, she feared for her safety with the Bishop still in the area.

"How…did you…get away?" Melody asked, coughing. "Where… is he?"

Lily shook her head. "He's gone; I don't know where he went."

Melody struggled to breathe; she'd known for several minutes that she could not move even her fingers. She cried out asking for safety for Lily and she was here with her now. Though she did not want to be alone because she sensed she was dying, she needed to be sure Lily was safe.

"Go… home," she said. "I don't…want him… to hurt… you." She coughed weakly.

Lily shook her head vigorously, sobs consuming her. "No, *Mamm;* I won't leave you."

"Tell…your…*daed* what…happened."

Lily wiped tears that dripped down the side of Melody's face, shushing her mother in between sobs.

Melody coughed again and felt something trickle down the side of her face.

Lily's eyes bulged. "*Mamm,* you're bleeding. Let me help you up; you have to see the doctor."

Melody's eyes filled with fresh tears; she knew she could not move, let alone, try to walk away from this accident. "*Nee,* I'm going…to be with…*Gott*. I can't…go with you."

"*Nee,* please don't leave me," Lily begged her.

Melody coughed harder, her breath hitching. "I...love…you."

"I love you too, *Mamm,"* Lily said, dropping her head to her mother's chest, sobbing even harder.

Melody breathed in the sweet smell of honeysuckle in her daughter's hair just before everything went black.

Chapter Three

Lily held her mother long after her heart stopped beating. She'd stopped sobbing, except for the occasional hitch in her breath, hoping to hear her mother's heartbeat once more. The sun was high overhead and it burned her skin, but she would not leave her mother's side.

Above her, on the bridge, clip-clop of horse's hooves clattered across the bridge. Lily's heart sped up; was the bad man with the black hat coming back to hurt her?

"Hello," a voice called out.

Did she know that voice? It was almost muffled, as if she was under water. She lifted her ear from her mother's heart and looked toward the bridge. The sun blinded her view of the person standing in the cutout window of the bridge.

"Lily," the voice called. "Melody—are you alright? Stay there, I'm coming down there."

"It's *Daed;* he's going to help you," Lily whispered.

She sucked in a breath and let it out with a burst of tears. Her father would make it right; he'd take her mother to the doctor and she would be alright.

Hurry, Daed.

She laid her head back down on her mother's chest and listened for her heart.

"Please come back," she cried. "*Daed* is coming and he'll help you."

She sobbed harder; she knew her mother wasn't coming back to her.

She knew.

Sam Fisher rushed down the ravine to get to his wife and daughter, slipping several times on the uneven terrain. How had they gotten down there? Every few feet, he looked down at them, and judging by his daughter's crying, something was seriously wrong.

"Melody," he called out to his wife.

Why wouldn't she answer him?

His heart beat hard against his chest wall, his breathing labored, as he made his way closer to them. Lily rested on her haunches, hovering over her mother and sobbing. Fear gripped him when he realized she could be severely hurt—or worse.

"Hurry, she needs you!" Lily cried out.

Sam looked up; he'd made it more than halfway down, but the worst rocky part was still between him and his family.

"Hang in there, Lily," he said, bending to brace his hands against the rocks to help him down. "How's your *mamm?*"

"She's bleeding," Lily called up to him. "She won't move."

Bleeding?

Won't move?

Had she fallen from the bridge? Judging from the way the buggy was wedged into the side of the bridge and where she lay on the ground—half in the creek, he imagined the worst.

Gott, give me the strength to face this trial.

With his back to his daughter, her crying became louder every step he took to reach her. He turned several times, nearly losing his footing, but the scene at the bottom of the creek bed was the same.

When he finally reached a spot where he could stand upright without grappling onto the grass and rocks, he hesitated before resuming his journey. He already knew his wife was dead; he could feel it in his soul. He bit back tears, knowing that to fall apart in front of Lily would not be good for her.

He would be strong—for Lily.

Before he reached his wife and daughter, someone from the bridge called out to him—an *Englisher*. "Do you need help?" the man asked, holding up his phone.

Sam stopped and nodded up toward the man, knowing he would need help getting his family back up the side of the ravine. "*Jah.*"

Then he collapsed next to his daughter, pulled her sobbing, shaky frame into one arm, and grabbed his wife's wrist with his other hand. He moved his fingers around in a panic; there was no pulse. Moving Lily over, he laid his head on Melody's chest to listen for her heartbeat.

He didn't find one.

His breath hitched, but he bit down hard on his cheek to keep his emotions in check; right now, his daughter needed him, and there was nothing to do for his beloved wife.

He picked up Lily, but she grappled onto her mother's light blue dress, clenching with iron fists.

"Let me stay with *Mamm,*" she screamed. "I have to protect her."

The more he tried to pull her away, the louder she screamed; it broke his heart.

He let her go and held her in one arm, and picked up his wife's hand, pulling it close to his cheek. Sobs caught in his throat, but he let them go; he just couldn't hold it in any longer.

It wasn't long before sirens reached his ears. Sam dried his face and wiped his nose on the sleeve of the blue, button-down shirt Melody had sewn for him. She'd always gotten after him for that; she'd pushed a handkerchief in the pocket of his broadfall pants every day hoping to tame his bad habit. He reached into his pocket, but there was no hanky; she must have forgotten today. She'd left the *haus* early to deliver fresh eggs to their neighbors, so they would have them for their Sunday morning meal before church service.

Why hadn't he stopped her? She'd pecked his lips with a quick kiss and then drove off with a smile and wave.

A rescue team was already lowering a rescue gurney from the side of the bridge with a wince, and paramedics were upon them. How had they gotten down the bottom of the ravine so quickly? Their voices were muffled in Sam's ears, and they prodded him with questions he couldn't comprehend.

When they tried moving Lily aside, she belted out a primal scream.

Sam snapped back to reality and scooped up his kicking and screaming daughter, pulling her away from her mother so the paramedics could put her on the stretcher.

They examined her body, shaking their heads, the hopeless looks on their faces stabbing at Sam's heart.

He held Lily tightly, so they could strap his wife to the blue, plastic stretcher, then they connected it to the cable and raised it up to the bridge. He turned Lily away so she wouldn't see what was happening to her mother, but she was so out-of-control, he could barely hold onto her. It frightened him that she could be so stricken with grief; he'd never seen her act out like this before.

A police officer approached him. "It looks like your horse must have been spooked—probably by a snake. By the looks of your buggy and the angle it's tipped backward, I'd say your wife was thrown clear from the seat and out the window. She appears to have died on impact, so I don't believe she suffered. I'm sorry for your loss." His voice was loud, and he spoke in choppy sentences in between Lily's cries.

Sam nodded mindlessly. At least she didn't suffer; he wished he could say the same for his daughter.

"After we get the pictures we need of the scene, we'll help you to get the buggy unhooked from the railing on the bridge;

hopefully, then your horse will calm down. He's pretty agitated."

Again, Sam nodded; there was nothing he could do or say to bring back his wife, and nothing that would calm his child or his own aching heart.

Chapter Four

Sam stood near his wife's grave, Lily at his side. She whimpered quietly while the Bishop spoke the eulogy. She hadn't spoken once in the past three days, and she'd barely eaten anything.

News of Melody's accident had made the front page of the newspaper, and plenty of *English* folks had come to the funeral to pay their respects.

Sam stared at the flowers that lay on Melody's casket; he'd picked them from her garden. In only one season, she'd planted a whole lifetime of flowers, nurturing the seedlings until they'd bloomed fully. She'd brought most of the clippings from the rose bushes from her own garden after the landlord had decided he no longer wanted to rent to them. With no parents to bequeath them property, they'd always rented, and Sam had finally earned enough to pay for a small mortgage. Being a harness maker wasn't the most profitable, but he'd used his skills to sell bridles to the western store in town, and that had made up the difference.

Now, he had no reason to build the house they'd dreamed about for so many years.

Lily clung to his side; what was he going to do with her? Melody had left him with no instructions. Even if she could have, he was still lost—especially since she hadn't spoken to him once since he allowed the paramedics to remove her mother's body from the ravine.

It had seemed like months had passed since that day; perhaps they were both still in shock from it, but he didn't know how he was going to function without her. Melody's cousin, Emily, had offered to come and help for a while, and he'd agreed, though he hadn't figured out how that was going to work out. He only prayed it would not be awkward being a guest in her own home; she'd been their landlord for the past year, and she'd been a good one, but this was different.

She was his wife's family—not his.

Would the Bishop approve of such an arrangement? Emily was a single woman, and now, he was a widower. Perhaps he should have checked with him first.

As the Bishop ended the funeral, the pallbearers began to lower Melody's casket into the ground. Sam felt Lily slip away from his side; her ear-piercing scream startled him, bringing his gaze in focus.

"Don't take her away from me!" Lily cried.

Lily had been to other funerals in the community; she knew enough about death to accept the routine of a funeral, didn't she?

Sam snapped out of his own thoughts and scooped up Lily the same way he'd had to at the edge of Peace Creek. Only now, the entire community and more was there to witness his child's breakdown. He wished he could spare her the hurt he, himself, was feeling, but there did not seem to be any reasoning with her.

He held her close and told her it was going to be alright.

"*Nee,*" she cried. "I need to tell her I'm sorry."

Sam's heart slammed against his ribcage, a million thoughts crowding his mind.

"What are you sorry for?" he asked in her ear. "This wasn't your fault."

It was a random accident and probably not preventable—unless she'd stayed home that morning. But that just wasn't in Melody's nature; she was always thinking of others above herself. She would only have stayed home that morning if he'd asked her to.

If anyone was to blame, it was him; he'd been too busy to hitch up the horse that morning, and Melody was too good-natured to pull him away from his work to ask for help. Perhaps if he'd helped her, the timing might have been different, and the horse might not have encountered whatever it was that had spooked him that morning.

"She told me to run and I didn't listen to her." Lily sobbed. "I should have run home and told you to help her. She told me to and I didn't mind her."

Sam pulled his daughter away from his shoulder to look into her eyes. "What are you talking about?"

"He killed her, and I didn't run to you for help."

"Chestnut didn't mean to hurt your *mamm,*" he said.

"Chestnut was scared," Lily said. "He scared him."

"Who?" Sam asked. "Who scared Chestnut?"

"I don't know his name." she cried. "*Mamm* told me to run and I didn't run. I'm sorry."

"What did he look like?"

"I'm sorry," she repeated.

"Was there someone there that day on the bridge?" Sam asked his daughter.

Lily screamed and buried her head in her father's shoulder.

"Tell me, Lily," he begged. "Did someone see what happened to your *mamm?*"

Lily lifted her head, her eyes glazed over with a fear he'd never seen in her.

"Red light—green light," she said.

"What are you talking about?"

"Green light—red light—green light."

Lily wouldn't stop repeating the phrase no matter how much he tried to reason with her. She said it loudly at first, until it turned into mumbles that were almost inaudible.

Sam carried her away from the funeral and back to the waiting buggy, patting Chestnut on the head before putting his delirious daughter in the back seat.

Chapter Five

Emily Yoder steered Molasses up to the new bridge that stretched across Peace Creek and pulled back suddenly on the reins.

"Whoa, Boy!"

The horse stopped with a jolt, causing her small buggy to wobble. Perhaps she'd pulled a little too hard, but her shaky hands couldn't be stilled.

The hair on the back of her neck stood on end. Could she cross this same bridge that had taken the life of her cousin, Melody? She feared this bridge for more reasons than her cousin's death. They'd ruled Melody's death as a freak accident, calling it the fault of the horse. Something had spooked that horse; Adam's ghost, perhaps? She didn't believe in all that stuff, but there was a lot of hushed talk in the community about it—especially after Lily's breakdown. She'd claimed there was a man who'd spooked the horse—not in so many words, but it was the conclusion.

She drew in a deep breath, hoping to calm her foolish thoughts.

Her heart raced at the thought of crossing the bridge, and she held her breath with a long gasp. It wasn't the same bridge that had claimed Adam's life, but it still crossed Dead Man's Ravine over the very spot where he'd fallen to his death a year ago. Now, with

Melody's death on the new bridge only a few days ago, the community was in a state of unrest.

She couldn't help but remember that night on the old bridge when Adam had tried to harm her and her twin sister, Eva. Though more than a year had passed, she could still hear the echo of Adam's scream as if it hung over the ravine like a thick fog; it haunted her.

She shivered from the early morning chill in the air; could she cross the new covered bridge? Immediately after Adam's accidental fall last year, the city had gone to work tearing down the narrow, one-lane bridge, and had constructed a wider bridge in its place. No, it wasn't the same bridge; it didn't even look the same. But since her cousin had fallen to her death, the ravine had claimed the lives of two people she knew.

Unfortunate for her, she needed to cross the bridge in order to reach her destination: her childhood home.

It was too late to go around the other way; Sam was expecting her.

Molasses whinnied and snorted, and bobbed his head up and down. Emily's heart drummed against her ribcage as she pulled the slack in the reins. "Whoa, Boy!" she called to him with a shaky voice.

Something had spooked him.

Gooseflesh tingled up her arms and ruffled the hair at the back of her neck.

She kept a tight hold of the reins.

Though the horse wasn't anxious to get across the bridge; she was. The horse had no real worries or bad memories of nearly being killed in this very spot. She'd been lucky that night that the same thing that had happened to her twin sister, Eva, had not happened to her.

So why was he so spooked? Was it the same thing that had spooked Melody's horse last week?

She'd attended the funeral in town at the cemetery yesterday, and that was the closest she'd come to this area of the community for a year. She'd been too shaken up to come back.

Cousin Alma had rented out Emily's childhood home to their cousin, Melody, and her family. Now that Melody's daughter was without a mother, she had agreed to take over her care. To do that, she needed to return to her home.

After what had happened on the bridge that night with Adam, she'd packed her things and left her home in the community to stay with Alma. Then, when Eva was near the end of her pregnancy, she stayed with her until she was back on her feet after the birth. She couldn't keep running from the past—and she couldn't let the random accident that happened to her cousin paralyze her.

I'm alright; I'm just spooked—like Molasses. I'm sure it's nothing.

The pep-talk she was giving herself wasn't making her limbs stop shaking. She had a bad feeling, but she had to get across the bridge. If she went around the long way, it would take her another thirty minutes, and she was already late. She'd promised to meet Sam, her cousin's widow, to go over everything she needed to know so she could keep Lily's routines as familiar as possible. The poor child had suffered a breakdown after seeing her mother thrown from the buggy and hadn't spoken a sensible word since.

At the funeral, she'd stared blankly the entire service, until they went to lower the casket into the grave. She'd screamed and thrown herself over the coffin and wouldn't let go until she was nearly passed out with exhaustion. The doctor had needed to sedate her to keep her from repeating the strange phrase that no one could figure out.

Emily shuddered just remembering what a scene the child had made, but truthfully, she'd wanted to do the same thing when her own mother had died. She hadn't been ready to let her go any more than she was ready to let her father go. She knew exactly how Lily felt, but the difference was, Lily was only a child; Emily's losses were more recent.

Was she prepared to handle such a troubled child?

Even if she wasn't, Lily was family, and for that reason, she would do all she could to help.

Emily rubbed her arms and hugged herself; could she allow Molasses to drive across the bridge while she kept her eyes closed? No; if he'd been on the bridge before she would trust him more, but this bridge was just as unfamiliar to him as it was to her.

Her gaze traveled the length of it; they'd made it somehow longer than the old bridge; it would take her a little longer to get across. She eyed the open window cutouts; it was rumored the city planned to enclose the openings with bars to prevent any more falls. A lot of good that would do her now; her buggy was just as open as Melody's, and her horse was more spirited than Chestnut. Naming her horse Molasses had been a joke; he did like to run when he wasn't supposed to.

Her first thought was to jump down and walk Molasses across; it was the only way she was going to get across, because she had no intention of dying today. If anyone should see her, would they think she was a fool, or would they understand?

Oh, what did she care for? It was her life! She was burning daylight sitting here trying to decide.

She hopped down from the buggy and grabbed onto the lead straps. She patted her horse on the side and set him at a slow walk. It was silly, and in her mind, she calculated how long it would take her to go around whenever she needed to go this direction, knowing it was necessary to visit Eva and her growing family. She supposed she'd have to cross it again when the opportunity presented itself, and perhaps, in time, she'd become more used to it. Today, she would walk, and her heart wouldn't beat normally again once the short journey ended.

Reconsidering her offer as a temporary nanny for eight-year-old Lily, Emily steered Molasses into the yard of her childhood home. It had been a long year since she'd rented the home out to the Fishers. It was only natural that she rent to Melody and her husband; it was best to keep her farm in the family until she was ready to live there again. Melody's death had made that decision for her. The strange accident had forced her to decide sooner than she'd planned, but sometimes it's best not to let old worries linger too long.

Naturally, Emily had offered her services as a caretaker at the funeral, and now she wondered if that was the best decision she could have made. She hadn't thought about how strange it would be to move back into her home until she sat here now staring at it.

If she'd known it would feel this foreign to her, she'd have backed out of her offer. She sighed heavily; going back on her word was not an option.

She climbed down from her buggy, wondering if Sam was in the house or the barn. Her gaze followed the trim yard and the newly-painted porch; Sam had done a lot of work to clean the place up. At the back side of the house, her mother's garden took her breath away.

A white, picket fence enclosed flowering plants and rose bushes in the most vibrant colors she'd ever seen. Butterflies fluttered above the plants, alighting on the colorful blossoms. A smile curved her lips; she knew her cousin kept a beautiful flower garden, but she never dreamed she'd plant such a beautiful garden out of the dead mess she'd left behind when she'd moved to the city with Alma.

Her gaze followed the trail of color until she noticed Lily standing among the plants. Her deep purple dress blended with the flowers and she almost didn't see her.

"Lily," she called out to her, but the girl did not turn around.

"Lily," she called again.

The child turned around and stared at her blankly. When Emily took a step toward her, Lily screamed and ran into the garden, hidden among the maze of plants.

Emily lifted her eyes and sighed.

Lord, give me strength; this isn't going to be easy.

Chapter Six

Emily followed Sam around her old house as he instructed her and *showed her around;* she humored him, knowing he wasn't in the best state of mind, and had probably forgotten that this was her house up until a year ago when he and Melody had moved in.

"I'm sorry about Lily," he said. "She and Melody spent the entire summer in that garden; I suppose she feels closest to her there. She won't let anyone in there—not even me!"

Emily felt helpless to save her cousin's child from the grief she likely didn't understand. "I'm sure in time…"

Sam nodded. "Well, I'm sure you don't need me to tell you how to run a *haus*—especially not this one. You already know where everything is. I'm sorry if I'm rambling, but this is awkward for me. You and I don't really know each other, but I know Melody would have trusted you to fill in for her with Lily in her absence."

He turned away from her and cleared his throat.

Emily felt sorry for him; it couldn't have been easy for him to say that, but she really appreciated it.

"Danki," she said.

She resisted the urge to place a comforting hand on his shoulder; he was only a couple of years older than she was, and a very handsome man at that. She did not want him

53

getting the wrong idea. She would save her comforting for Lily—if she would let Emily get anywhere near her, that is.

He coughed and cleared his throat again before facing her. "I know it's late, but I couldn't get Lily to eat anything; perhaps you could fix her a little snack and leave it on the table near the garden. They used to have tea and cookies out there."

She held a hand up to stop him; he was getting too choked up and she didn't want him torturing himself like that. Melody had been a lucky woman to have a man love her that way. She didn't think she'd ever get a chance to marry; Adam had been her only hope, and that had not ended well for her. The only good thing that had come from Adam was her niece, Faith.

Eva had gotten lucky with Ben; would marrying a widower be her only hope for marriage too? She shook the thought from her head; she was not there to marry Sam, she was there to take care of her cousin's daughter. Shame on her for letting her mind wander to such prideful thoughts.

"I'm afraid my only experience is with my sister, Eva's, toddlers," Emily offered, hoping it would change the subject enough to calm his worries.

"My Lily is acting like one for the past few days, so that might make it easier for you to handle her," he said quietly. "I want you to take care of her as if she was your own *kinner;* she doesn't have a *mamm* anymore, so she'll need one."

How long was Sam planning on having her stay; until Lily was grown up? She'd be a spinster by then. Surely, he didn't mean for her to raise her cousin's daughter. He was grieving, so she would not try to read anything into his words.

A knock at the door interrupted the awkward silence between them, and Emily was grateful. Donning an apron, she set to work on a snack for her and Lily while Sam went to the front door to answer it. Low voices made their way to the kitchen; it was the newly-appointed Bishop Yoder, whom Emily had not yet met. He'd taken Bishop Byler's place after he'd gone to jail last year.

Sam brought him into the kitchen and introduced him. He seemed like a pleasant sort of man, but he seemed troubled about something.

"Melody was your cousin?" he asked a bit sternly.

She nodded. "*Jah.*"

"So, then you're not related to Samuel?"

She shook her head.

What was with all the questions; she had a child to care for and didn't have time to answer the same questions reworded.

"You're here to care for the wee one?"

She busied herself after nodding again, hoping he would get the message.

"Where will you be staying?"

She knew now what he was getting at. Sam had offered to move his things out of the main house and stay in the *dawdi haus* so she would be there for Lily. She knew the rules about having an escort for such an extended stay.

Sam spoke up and relayed the sleeping arrangements.

He shook his head. "*Nee,* that isn't *gut* enough," he said. "I understand this is legally your home, but you cannot stay on the same property with a widower, especially since you're an unmarried woman."

57

Emily bit back the urge to talk back to the Bishop; she would let Sam handle it. They were men and she need not put herself in the position to make herself look bad on a first meeting with the new Bishop.

"I'm afraid your community standing is already under review after Lily's behavior at Melody's funeral service," he said sternly. "When it comes up that you have willingly entered into such an agreement with regard to your living arrangement, I'm afraid I have no choice but to insist you must marry. Otherwise, you cannot reside on the same property. You know the rules—both of you."

Sam pursed his lips. "The grass has not even grown over Melody's grave and you're talking marriage to me?"

Emily felt her heart thump; she was mourning for her cousin, but not nearly in the same way Sam must be. She could not marry her husband; it would feel like a betrayal.

Surely, Sam would agree with that.

"Don't think of it in that way," the Bishop said. "It must be a marriage of convenience—for the sake of your *dochder*. She needs a *mudder.*"

"*Jah,* I agree," Sam said.

What?! How can you agree with the Bishop? He's wrong!

"You can still take your mourning period," the Bishop said. "You can even stay out in the *dawdi haus* the way you'd planned, but in the eyes of the community, you've done the right thing and married her to take care of your *dochder.*"

Emily didn't dare turn around; they were talking about her as if she was not even there— and as if she had no say-so on the matter. It was not fair to any of them to agree to such an arrangement in order for Lily to be taken care of.

Sam was not answering the Bishop; Emily could feel the heat rising in her cheeks.

"I can marry you both now since you've taken the baptism, and we can keep it quiet until I can make an announcement at the services tomorrow," he said. "At that time, I will announce the marriage to the community to avoid giving anyone the chance to start any rumors."

Still no answer from Sam.

"I know this is a tough decision, but I'm sure you'll agree it's the only one to be made under the circumstances. You know if the situation were reversed, I'd be here advising the same thing to your widow."

What a harsh and cold thing to say!

Emily was fuming; she wanted Sam to make him leave, to tell him that community standing was not as important as healing from such a loss as he'd suffered.

And what of Lily? Doesn't she have a say in getting a new *mamm?* Emily hadn't even had the chance to get too near her without her getting spooked and running from her; how was she going to react when she finds out her mother has been replaced so quickly?

Emily couldn't quiet her mind; she was tempted to speak all of it to the Bishop, but it wasn't her place. It was Sam's—so why was he not speaking up?

The Bishop sighed at Sam's hesitation.

"If you don't marry Emily, she'll have to leave at once, and you'll have no one to care for Lily."

"Jah, I'll marry her," Sam said with a sigh.

What? Don't I get a say-so?

It took every bit of strength Emily had in her not to turn around and leave the house, but

she had to remember she was there for Lily—
not for Sam!

Chapter Seven

He'd pressed a brief kiss to her cheek and thanked her for agreeing to marry him! Never had she thought she would be thanked at her wedding by her groom; it wasn't every girl's idea of a dream wedding. She couldn't change the facts; she was married—in name only.

Her cheek was still warm where he'd kissed her, and that bothered her just a little bit.

Her heart fluttered around in her chest as if it was trying to beat, but it was lost in emotion—emotions Emily could not put a name to. If she had to guess, she'd call it shame, or embarrassment, or perhaps regret.

She was stuck! This was it—until death parted them.

There hadn't been time to change her clothes or to talk to Eva or Alma first. More than that—there hadn't been time to change her mind.

She'd said a brief prayer, but her mind was too cluttered to know if God had answered her or not, and she might have mistaken Sam's willingness as God's will.

What had she done?

The bishop had left as swiftly as he'd whirled in, and Sam was back out in the barn working as if nothing had happened. She bit back tears; it was her wedding day—a wedding without love.

She was thankful Lily had not interrupted their impromptu kitchen-wedding ceremony. If she could call it that. He'd avoided all the sentimental words and gotten right to the vows; it had not lasted more than three minutes, and it was over.

She was married!

She leaned over the sink and tried to calm the queasiness in her stomach. Eva had married for convenience, but she'd had the time to grow her love for Ben first. Albeit, they hadn't had long together first, but surely longer than the time she'd been in Sam's company. She hadn't been there more than an hour before the Bishop was demanding they make a lifetime commitment to one another.

Oh no! Was she about to be sick?

Was she being punished by God, Himself, for thinking Sam was a handsome widower?

Ach, Lord, forgive me. If we've acted in haste, please help us to find a way to make it work. Put love in my heart for that mann, and soften his heart toward me, even if he can never love me. I can live with him if he's a gentle mann...Lord, help me to calm down and come to terms with this. And bless Lily so she can accept it. Help me not to think selfish thoughts.

It was tough not to think selfish thoughts; she was, after all married, and had lost the stigma of dying a spinster. She was also a mother—something she never thought she would be. She'd always dreamed of it, but never dared to hope for such a thing to avoid being disappointed in her life. The likelihood of her having her own child was not very high, but she'd make Melody proud and be the best mother she could be to Lily.

Speaking of Lily; she took in a deep breath and blew it out slowly, and then went about the task of cutting up a fresh apple, thinking some berries would be nice to make some tarts. She knew Melody was famous for her berry tarts, and she had a feeling she may be able to win a little favor with Lily if she made her some. Her cousin had taught her how to make them, teasing her recently at Eva's house that they would help her to get a husband; if she only knew Emily was thinking of making some for *her* family, she might be unhappy with her.

Was such a thing possible? Would Melody look down from Heaven and be unhappy with her? Or was Heaven truly as grand as the Bible says, and she would be too happy walking streets paved with gold and living in the presence of God to pay any attention to the things that worry a woman here on earth?

She shook away her foolish thoughts; Sam would never be a real husband to her. The best she could hope for would be that the other women in the community would not spread rumors about her fake marriage.

No woman likes to be married out of obligation; it would pour salt in the wound if the women in the community suspected there was no hope for a real marriage between them. It was bad enough she thought it herself. She would be the perfect Amish *fraa* for Sam and the perfect *mamm* to Lily.

The kitchen door burst open and it startled Emily.

"*Mamm,*" Lily said, staring blankly. "I need you! Come quick!"

Had Sam told her about them getting married? Surely, Lily wouldn't call her *Mamm* already.

"What do you need, Lily?" Emily asked.

Lily turned her head, paused, and then squealed. Then, she ran out the door, sobbing as if she'd just remembered her mother was gone.

Emily put a hand over her heart, her breath catching in her throat. That child was going to take five years off her life every time she saw her if she didn't find a way to break her of the screaming habit. Sam had told her that it was new since the accident, and he'd even said she'd done the same thing to him, so she tried not to take it personally, and remember she was just a child.

She took another deep breath and finished preparing the snack that she prayed Lily would eat.

Chapter Eight

Emily readied herself for church early, so she could cook a proper breakfast; she would have to cook in her apron to keep her plain dress from getting dirty. Last night's dinner had been a disaster; luckily, there was still plenty of casseroles left over from the funeral and she hadn't had to make too much effort.

Getting Lily to sit at the table had been another story; Sam had reprimanded her more than once to sit still and eat after she pushed her food around her plate so much it ended up all over the table, and then when she shoved her plate and spilled her milk—that had been the last straw for poor Sam's nerves, and it was the end of Emily's good dress. With milk down the front of her church dress, she'd washed it and hung it up, hoping it would dry by morning, but it hadn't. She'd had to put on a work dress to wear to the service.

After making his daughter leave the table to go to her room, she'd fallen asleep in her clothes and without a bath. Emily laid awake most of the night in her childhood bedroom praying that the whole idea of her being here hadn't been a mistake. It was too late for wondering; she was married, and like it or not, she was now Lily's mother.

This morning, Lily resisted every effort Emily made to get her ready, but she was persistent. She'd run a bath for her and set out her clothes; she'd done everything short of putting Lily in the bathtub—in her nightgown, but that was next if she didn't mind. She'd been raised with discipline, and by the way Sam had handled her last night over the dinner fiasco, she was certain he would not object to her being strict with her parenting measures.

He'd told her to treat Lily as if she was her mother, and tossing her in the tub in her nightgown was certainly something Melody would do with her unruly child.

What she couldn't figure out about Lily was why she was acting up toward her—they'd always gotten along so well at family functions. She would probably understand it more if she'd never met Lily before, but she'd been a regular part of her life. All that knowledge did not help her to understand the child now. She'd changed; something had happened to her out there on the bridge— something more than just watching her mother killed. Something had shaken her to her very core, and Emily was bound and determined to find out what it was. If she couldn't, she wasn't sure Lily would ever be the same.

Emily stood outside Lily's door, but before she knocked, she could hear her inside the room.

"Red light—green light."

What does that mean?

She knocked, interrupting the child.

"Go away," Lily yelled.

"I ran bath water for you," Emily said as calmly as possible. "When you finish, your *vadder* expects you downstairs for breakfast."

There it was; she was putting the responsibility on Sam. It was the only leverage she had to use against the child. She didn't want to be too stern with her. She was suffering heartache and mourning the loss of her mother, but if she let the backtalk go on too long, it would become a regular habit, and that was not acceptable behavior.

Surely, the Bishop would put them under the ban if they could not get Lily's tantrums under control. Under normal circumstances, by Amish standards, she was too old to be acting out in such a way, but she would discuss with Sam how long he would let it go on. The Bishop had warned him to get Lily under control or he'd have to put a temporary ban on them, which would prevent them from coming to church and participating in social functions until he could prove Lily's outbursts were restrained.

Emily went back downstairs to finish the breakfast since all she'd done was to put some fresh cinnamon rolls in the oven. She would leave Lily alone to bathe and dress while she cooked up some ham slices and scrambled some eggs.

Moments later, Lily entered the kitchen and plopped down at the table.

Emily turned from the stove and saw that she was still in her nightgown and hadn't even combed her hair.

"Go take a bath and get dressed for church, Lily," Emily said.

She shook her head.

Emily pointed upward. "Go, now; you will not be permitted to eat until you're ready for church."

Lily folded her arms over her chest and furrowed her brow.

"Lily, go upstairs and take a bath, or you'll miss breakfast and you'll have to go to church dirty and hungry—and in your nightgown."

"You're not my *mudder*," Lily said.

"Yes, she is, Lily," Sam said as he entered the kitchen from the back door.

Emily's heart jumped. She kept to herself and continued to crack eggs into a bowl, her back to Sam.

"She is your *mudder* now, and you will mind her. Go get your bath and be dressed and ready for the meal, and you better hurry or you'll go to church with an empty belly."

Lily let out a loud cry, continuing to sob as she went upstairs, stomping on each step along the way.

Emily turned to speak to Sam, but he'd disappeared from the room.

Her heart raced, and her breathing quickened. Tears rolled down her cheeks, and she wiped them away with the back of her hand.

Why had God put such a burden on her?

Chapter Nine

The ride to the new Bishop's house was quiet; Sam had gone the long way around to avoid having to go on the bridge. She appreciated it, knowing it would likely upset Lily. She supposed it would probably hurt Sam too, but she suspected he did it more for Lily's sake than his own.

They arrived in plenty of time; several families arrived at the same time they did. Her heart thumped; there would be questions from members of the community—lots of questions. Questions she wasn't prepared to answer; should she have given potential questions a little more thought to keep from getting caught off guard?

It was too late to worry about it now. The Hochstetler family pulled up their buggy next to theirs. Linda had married Jeremy right after they'd turned eighteen and they had four young children already.

The men shook hands and Linda approached her. "I didn't know you were staying on," she said. "I thought you were only staying for a short visit."

"She's going to stay," Sam said, stepping in to save her from stumbling over an answer to an awkward question.

She supposed they would all be awkward for a while.

"Where are you staying? I'd love to visit with you," Linda asked.

"I'm staying at my house," she answered without thinking.

She hadn't meant to blurt it out, and judging by the drop of Linda's jaw and the bulging of her eyes, she was just as shocked as the Bishop had been when he was told.

"What will the Bishop say when he finds out?"

"We were married yesterday," Sam said, his voice cracking.

He said it a lot easier than she would have been able to.

Linda sucked in her breath, but quickly covered her mouth to cover her shock.

Emily watched Lily fidget and pull on Sam's arm to get his attention, but he ignored her. She was worried the child was going to make a scene over Sam's comment, and she was not prepared to handle any outbursts in front of everyone. She had no idea how other parents handled that from toddlers, but from an eight-year-old, it would be looked upon with disdain. Thankfully, Sam continued to ignore her erratic behavior until it was time to go inside the house for the service.

They stepped inside the door and Sam peeled Lily off his arm. "You sit with Katie over there; you see her—she's with her *mamm.*"

Lily shook her head and frowned, whimpering quietly.

Emily's heart sped up.

Please, Gott, calm Lily's mind and help her to sit apart from her vadder.

Sam took her hand and tucked it into Emily's and then walked up toward the front of the room where the Bishop stood and said a few words to him. Then he sat on the right side with what seemed to be a few friends.

Lily stood next to her with her arms folded and a scowl on her face.

"Shall we sit?" she said to Lily.

The girl snatched her hand away and walked over to her friend, Katie. Little did she know that Emily knew her mother, Lydia. They'd gone to school together.

She followed Lily, and the girl flashed her a scowl and then sat with a harrumph next to Katie.

Lydia stood to greet Emily. "I see she's having a bit of rebellion toward you," she whispered.

Emily nodded and sighed.

"The best way to handle that is to ignore her and pretend you don't notice when she's acting that way; she's trying to get a reaction out of you, I think."

"Sam was ignoring her outside, and I suppose he already knows how to handle her, but I don't want to upset her."

Lydia shook her head. "That's the wrong attitude," she said. "The Bishop told us he married you two yesterday; I know it's hard filling Melody's shoes, but don't try. You do need to show her you're the parent—and her authority now. I know she's been through a traumatic thing, but she still needs discipline."

"I'm hoping she's going to accept me as time wears on," Emily said with a discouraging sigh.

Lydia smiled. "Trust me; the first time she needs you for something, she'll be over the attitude!"

"I pray you're right."

"We're neighbors, now," Lydia said. "We bought the old Bontrager place, so if you ever need anything, we aren't too far away. The girls meet between the properties and play almost every day. Jeremy made them a tree *haus* in the big oak tree; you can always find them there."

"That's *gut* to know if I'm ever looking for her." Emily smiled and sat next to Lydia to wait for the service to begin.

Chapter Ten

Sam watched Emily from the other side of the Bishop's yard, where she and the other women were setting up food on the tables for the shared meal after church. It was such a lovely day; it was tough to grieve on such a day. The warm, Indian summer breeze clapping the already turning leaves together made him appreciate that he was alive. Melody loved the change of seasons, and the house was always filled with the aroma of pumpkin bread.

Would Emily make pumpkin bread?

He felt sorry for her; he knew she'd sacrificed a lot more than most women would. To take on the burden of an instant child and a husband in name only had to put a strain on her. He wouldn't know it by looking at her smile; it was as fresh as the morning dew.

It had been a long church service today, and with the awkward announcement of their impromptu marriage, she seemed to be holding up better than he was. He'd glanced back at her a few times and was happy to see Lily sitting quietly next to her. It was a relief to him that she didn't make a scene like she had at the funeral. Perhaps she would calm down after some time had passed, the way the doctor had advised him.

Now, as he watched Emily, he couldn't help but notice how truly beautiful she was.

The breeze played with her blonde curls that had somehow escaped her prayer *kapp,* and her smile had not wavered. She seemed content to work alongside the women in the community, but she'd grown up with them, and it would be easy for her to fit back in.

He knew of the stories for the reasons behind her leaving the community; it was the reason he and Melody had rented her house. He worried some would pass rumors that he married her partly to stake a claim on her house, but it wasn't true. He'd only thought of his precious child without a mother. He'd spent many hours awake wondering if the decision he'd made was the right one, and he'd not given poor Emily much of a choice.

But watching her now as she cared for his daughter, he could only pray that in time he would be able to love her the way she deserved. She was a good woman, though he didn't know her very well, personally. Melody had always spoken very highly of her. Though it had not been an easy one, he was pleased with his decision to marry Emily.

Emily could feel Sam's eyes on her; it made her a little uncomfortable—as if she was being scrutinized. She prayed she was wrong, but she was embarrassed she wasn't able to control the child that was now hers. She wasn't certain what he expected from her, but she was feeling a little inadequate as a mother and a wife—both of which were nothing short of a big charade.

She'd put a letter in the mail to Eva, hoping to get some advice and even a visit. She knew it was a long trip with two little ones, but she needed her sister now more than anything. Lydia's offer had been kind, but it wasn't the same as having her sister to talk to about her troubles. She would likely be shocked at the marriage that was so soon it was almost scandalous. In her defense, it hadn't been her idea. She only prayed God would put love in her heart for the man, so she could one day be a wife to him if he'd have her as such.

The quiet ride home from the service seemed long; at least Lily was sleeping peacefully in the back seat of the open buggy. She'd worn herself out playing, and Emily had been happy to see her playing. She'd even caught her smiling once, but when their eyes met, the scowl returned. If Melody were here, she'd be able to tell her what to do, but she remained as quiet as possible in Sam's presence, not wanting to burden him further with her feelings of inadequacy at being an instant parent.

There was so much she'd wanted to ask Sam, but she felt awkward. Even now, sitting beside him in the buggy, their thighs bumped every time they hit a little bump in the road, and it caused her cheeks to heat with embarrassment.

Would it always be this way?

When they pulled into the yard, Sam halted the horse and hopped down to assist her out of the buggy. It was a sweet gesture, but it brought more heat to her cheeks. She turned away and cleared her throat when Sam hesitated before letting go of her waist. She wished her marriage could be under better circumstances, but God had put her in this one for a reason, and she would wait for Him to show her why.

Lily startled her by jumping out of the buggy and running toward the garden.

"You have chores to do, Lily, don't forget that," Sam hollered after her.

She waved a hand behind her without looking back, and Sam let out a heavy sigh.

Emily touched his arm lightly, the warmth of it sending prickles of heat all the way to her elbow.

"I know it's a small consolation," she said. "But she probably needs a break from behaving so well today."

He nodded and flashed her a half-smile.

"You're probably right; hold her accountable though," he urged her. "Make sure she feeds the chickens and gathers the afternoon eggs."

Emily forced a weak smile, thinking that it would be so much easier if she would just take care of the chore herself, but it was Lily's responsibility. "I will."

Chapter Eleven

Emily opened the door to find Katie standing there with a basket in her hands.

"*Mamm* sent these over to you; she thought you could probably use some help," she said matter-of-factly.

She took the basket and lifted the linen towel and was delighted and relieved to see two freshly-baked loaves of bread.

Was she that obviously inadequate as a parent and wife? She'd been there a couple of weeks already and hadn't been able to get caught up on anything. Dinner was always late, the wash was not being done all in one day, and she'd begun to get a little discouraged.

She took the basket over to the counter and bent to breathe in the aroma. She loved smelling freshly-baked bread when it filled the house, but she hadn't done much baking since she'd been back in her own kitchen.

Truth was, she'd gotten behind in her bread-baking and everything else since she'd taken on the full-time job of parenting and doing double chores. Lily had been slacking in hers, and she'd been picking up the slack for two reasons. She was hoping to give Lily a break and let her know she'd do anything for her, and she was trying not to look like a failure in Sam's eyes.

It didn't help matters that she'd been preoccupied with thoughts of wanting to be a real wife to Sam. They'd had plenty of awkward glances and accidental touches in the past few days, and she was beginning to wonder if a friendship might be blossoming between them. He'd become more talkative and inviting of companionship if nothing else.

Emily smiled at Katie. "Tell your *mamm danki* for me."

"I need the basket back so Lily and I can go pick blueberries."

Emily snapped away from the mesmerizing scent of the bread and focused on Katie. "Where are you picking blueberries?"

Katie pointed in the direction of the patch she knew well; it stood between her property and Bishop Byler's property.

Her heart sped up at the thought of the girls wandering that close to the unstable man.

Lily came bouncing into the kitchen, her hair in blond braids that hung just over her collarbones, her prayer *kapp* lopsided on her head. At least she was wearing it; Emily had bigger things to worry about, and let it go for the time being.

"Are you ready to pick blueberries?" Katie asked Lily.

The child smiled and nodded eagerly.

Emily sighed; this was going to hurt.

"I'm sorry," she said. "But you can't go, Lily, and I don't think you should go either, Katie."

Lily stamped her foot on the floor and folded her arms in front of her, the scowl Emily had begun to become familiar with forming on her face.

"Why?" she demanded.

"I don't want you venturing off too far from home."

It was a weak excuse, and judging by the child's growing anger in her eyes, she contemplated telling her the truth instead of giving her an excuse.

Truth was, Emily knew that patch of blueberries well. She and Eva used to pick the berries for their mother every summer. It was how they'd come to know Adam so well.

"We always go there," Katie said. "It's not too far."

It wasn't the distance that had her worried. Since the ladies at church had confirmed that the Bishop was indeed back on the property on house-arrest, she had no idea what his boundaries entailed; it was too much of a risk to think that he might not be able to wander around his own property, and that large patch of blueberries bordered both properties.

She had to assume they would allow him to work his land, and that would mean the girls might encounter him. She had no idea what he was capable of after he was arrested at Eva's house trying to see her *boppli*.

"Does your *mamm* know you were planning on going there to pick them?" Emily asked.

She shrugged. "She doesn't care."

"Well, I *do* care, and I'm asking you not to go over there anymore."

Lily stomped her foot again. "*Mamm* always let me go!"

"Well, that was before…" Emily stopped mid-sentence, not wanting to finish.

"I know," Lily said with a raised voice. "My *mamm*'s dead!"

That's not what she was going to say, but she could see how Lily might have taken it that way. She just didn't want them around the Bishop; if he wasn't home on house-arrest, it would be a different story. He wasn't stable and couldn't be trusted.

Lily began to cry. "I want some tarts—I want my *mudder.*"

"I'm sorry," Emily bent to hug Lily, but the child pushed her away and ran out the kitchen door.

She sighed and looked at Katie, who seemed spooked by the whole incident.

She turned to leave.

"Hold on a minute, Katie," she said as calmly as possible. "I'd like you to take your *mamm* a note for me, would you please?"

She nodded, but went over and stood by the door.

Emily quickly grabbed a pencil and a small pad of paper from the counter and wrote out a note explaining everything to her; surely, Lydia would agree with her reason for keeping the girls from that berry patch. At least she prayed it was so.

When she finished, she folded it up, praying the girl could not yet read cursive writing; she knew Lydia could because they'd attended school together.

"Take that to your *mudder* and ask her to send me back a reply," Emily instructed her.

She took the note and nodded, and then was out the door.

Emily watched from the kitchen window to make sure they were going back in the direction of Katie's farm instead of the opposite way toward the Byler farm. Relief filled her when Katie ran across the field toward her house, Lily close on her heels.

Chapter Twelve

Emily straightened up the living room and dusted the furniture. In the corner, the large trunk with Melody's sewing in it was wide open, most of the materials in piles on the floor beside it. She and Lily made dolls and had sold them at their roadside stand, along with baked goods, fresh vegetables, and flowers from the garden. She supposed Lily was lost without that routine with her mother now that she was gone.

She picked up a male doll that she'd seen Lily working on the past couple of weeks and examined it. She'd fashioned his broadfall pants and made little suspenders, and added a white, yarn beard. When had she done that?

She wondered why she would make an older doll when most of the dolls that were still unfinished seemed to be young females, except for two that had brown beards. It struck her as odd, and something about it didn't feel right, but she couldn't put her finger on it. She brushed it aside, figuring Melody must have made a variety of dolls, even though she'd never seen any of them. The only ones she'd seen at the roadside stand had been sets of younger, *courting* couples.

She tossed it in the cedar chest along with the rest of the materials and went about finishing the basic cleanup. She'd left most of her family furniture in the house when she'd rented the house to Sam and Melody, so it was a little odd taking care of the home as the lady of the house.

She wished Lily would let her in her little world she was slowly closing herself up in, but the child hadn't spoken to her in more than a week. She'd been so angry about the note she'd sent to Lydia warning her to keep the girls away from the blueberry patch, she hadn't uttered even a word to her—not even to give her backtalk. It had been a quiet week, but at least when she was giving her backtalk, there was communication to build on.

The house had been silent, but she still wasn't doing her chores. She'd made one mess after another, and like now, with her sewing, Emily was picking up the slack and covering for her. She had a feeling Lydia would advise her not to do it, to let Lily get into trouble with her father, but Emily just didn't have the heart to do it. She could sense something was terribly wrong in Lily's world and she needed time to gain her trust; she truly thought that if she coddled Lily that she would eventually give in to her conscience and let Emily in.

Sam came in for lunch just as she was putting away the last of the things and closed the lid on the cedar chest. She turned around quickly at the noise, her hand flying up over her heart. He'd startled her.

He stood there for a minute, which made her nervous; had she done something wrong?

"How long are you going to keep doing Lily's chores?" he asked, suppressing a smile.

"I suppose that depends on how long you've known about it," she answered, teetering on her heels.

"I know you're trying to take it easy on Lily, but Melody was stricter than I am. You're not doing the child any favors—or yourself, for that matter, by trying to be her friend. She needs a *mudder*—she has Katie to be her friend."

Emily nodded, but it was tough for her to keep her concentration. She noticed his gaze travel to her lips a couple of times; did he want to kiss her? Adam had done that before he'd kissed her for the first time. If he tried, did she want Sam to kiss her?

She did.

She'd been daydreaming too much about it—so much so, that she'd prayed almost day and night to keep her growing attraction toward Sam from burning her up with desire for him. She'd felt guilty for wanting a real marriage, but she would never make an advance toward him. If it was something he wanted, he would have to make the move.

"I believe in you, Emily," he said, gently. "You've been a *gut mamm* to her."

Her cheeks heated, and her gaze fell to the floor. "*Danki.*"

He closed the space between them and tucked his finger under her chin, lifting gently. Her heart sped up and her knees felt wobbly at his touch. His fingers explored her neck, sending shivers of excitement through her like falling embers from a lit sparkler when twirled on a warm summer night.

She extended her chin, exposing more of the flesh on her neck, allowing him to prod a little more. Her lips parted as he dipped his face toward hers, her breath held in.

His lips brushed gently against hers, causing her to moan slightly when she exhaled. Her hands went around his neck and her fingers raked through his hair, pulling him closer as she deepened the kiss.

A high-pitched scream from Lily rent the air, breaking the spell between them.

Emily broke her grasp on Sam and stepped back; breathless, she made eye-contact with Lily only long enough to see the tears welling up in her eyes. She took a step toward her, but Lily backed, turned around, and ran from the room, sobbing.

Emily started to go after her, but a firm hand on her arm stopped her. "Let her have some space; she's no more used to seeing us in an embrace than I am in being in the middle of it."

Oh no, did he regret kissing me?

"I think we're all going to need some time to get used to things," he said.

He bent and kissed her on the cheek and left the room; Emily collapsed onto the sofa after she heard the back door close, and wept quietly.

Chapter Thirteen

Lily finished pushing the sticks into the ground that outlined her makeshift bridge in the corner of her mother's garden. Then she placed the Bishop doll she'd sewn behind the sticks.

She wagged her finger at the doll. "You stay there where you can't hurt my *mudder!*"

Picking up her berry pail, she stood and watched the doll for a minute. "Don't you move!" she said to it.

After a few minutes, she broke her gaze on the doll and went off in the direction of the field to pick some blueberries for a make-believe tea party in the garden with her mother.

She headed out toward the field that separated their farm from the next one. She swung her tin, shallow pail by the handle as she walked through the meadow of alfalfa and clover that would soon be ready for the next cutting and baling. The thin, green blades swayed in the breeze, tickling her as she walked through it; in some spots, it was as tall as she was.

Her father had let the mowing go for longer than he should have for the final baling, but come winter, it would be in the barns of most of the community. Even she knew some of that money would fund a meager Christmas for her; that meant sugary confections in her stocking that would hang from the fireplace, perhaps a store-bought book to read, or a new pair of ice skates since she'd outgrown her other pair.

She put away the whimsical thoughts of the upcoming season and worried about gathering the last of the berries before the first frost would take them.

When she reached the berry patch, she filled her pail quickly, but decided to indulge in a few before she left the patch of overgrown bushes. She set her pail down on the ground, so she could grab them with both hands. They were so tasty, and she'd missed the afternoon meal because she was hiding.

The snap of a twig pricked her ears at the same time a shadow loomed over her. Her gaze lifted from the blueberry bushes; the sun was behind him and cast a shadow over his angry face, but she knew him.

The berries in her hands dropped slowly to the ground and she swallowed hard the mouthful she'd been chewing on, nearly choking on it. Her gaze fell to her pail on the ground at her feet, but her focus was on the green light that turned red when he took a step toward her.

Red light—green light.

"I remember you," he said with a crooked, half-smile. "I told you we'd meet again."

He was the man from the bridge.

She eyed her pail of berries; could she snatch the pail without him grabbing for her? She knew he couldn't reach her without the mechanical device on his ankle turning red; did it hurt him when it was red?

Although he couldn't go any further in the field, the pail was between them, and he could reach the pail.

"I warned you, didn't I?" he asked, grabbing for her arm. He caught her wrist and he teetered over the edge, his alarm blinking red and beeping.

Lily squealed; she fought him, twisting her arm, but he was too strong. He scooped her up by her waist and hung her at his side, his other hand over her mouth to quiet her. She wriggled and cried, but he had her muzzled while he walked back toward his barn with her.

Emily searched all over the house for Lily, looking in the empty barn, and had even walked through the tall grass between the properties to look in the tree house. She wasn't anywhere to be found. She'd called for her at the edge of the deep flower garden, and she'd contemplated Lily was ignoring her; now she was certain of it.

There was simply nowhere else she could be. It dawned on her that Lily could be hiding from her because of what happened earlier between her and Sam, but if she didn't find her soon, she'd begin retracing her steps until she did.

When she reached the garden, she called for Lily, but she didn't answer. Panic filled her; was the child playing games with her, or possibly trying to get her into *trouble* with Sam? He'd gone into town for supplies, and it was the first time he'd left her alone with Lily, and she was failing at being a mother— miserably failing at it.

Tears welled up in her eyes, and a lump constricted her throat. Why would Lily run off if not to rebel even more? In the weeks that she'd been with them, the child had done nothing but rebel against her. She refused to do her chores, and so Emily had done them for her to make Sam think she had everything under control. She'd pretty much let the child run amuck, and it was wearing thin on her nerves. When he'd called her out for it and kissed her, she thought things were looking up—until Lily caught them off guard. Her tantrum and now her disappearance filled Emily with a feeling of dread.

She stood in front of the garden and called for her again, listening for any movement.

Nothing but silence, except for the rustling of the late summer leaves blowing in the cool breeze. The sun was sinking fast, and Emily knew if she didn't find Lily soon, it would be too dark to look.

Gott, please help me find her. Be with her and give her wisdom and courage. Let her know I love her—as my own dochder.

Tears ran down her cheeks; it was the first time she realized she truly loved Lily—

and Sam; she couldn't bear to lose his child any more than he could.

She had to find Lily—quickly.

Lily couldn't breathe around the hand that covered her mouth. Her stomach ached where his arm was wrapped around her like a sack of grain. Tears dripped from her eyes and mucous blew out of her nose in bubbles as she tried to breathe. She bounced around in his arms as he trudged across the uneven field; it was giving her a stomach ache and caused her to gag on the berries souring in her nervous stomach.

She tried to scream, but his hand clamped down on her face so hard it made her jaw ache. Fear of this man consumed her; she couldn't breathe.

She'd been so angry with her *vadder,* and determined to have her own way, that she hadn't even told Cousin Emily—her new *mamm,* where she was going.

No one would come looking for her.

"Let—me—go," she screamed around the fingers digging into her cheeks.

"I can't let you go; you saw what happened on the bridge," he said.

Tears ran down her face. "I won't—tell—anyone," she cried around his strong hand covering her mouth.

"I'm going to bury you behind the barn, so you can be with your *mudder.*"

Lily's heart raced, and her blood ran cold; her eyes rolled back as she gave up her fight, and everything went black.

Chapter Fourteen

Emily ventured into the garden, calling out for Lily. Something at the far corner caught her eye, and she stepped cautiously toward it, unsure of what to make of it.

Behind a row of sticks poking into the dirt, was the old Amish doll with the white beard. Her heart flip-flopped when she noticed the black hat and coat. Only one man dressed like that in the community; Bishop Byler.

Had she seen him since he'd been out of jail?

Emily picked up the doll, her blood running cold when she noticed the band around the doll's ankle. She moved it closer to get a better look at it; Lily had used her crayons to draw a red and green dot on the band.

Red light—green light!

Oh no! Gott, please, no!

A high-pitched scream raised the hair on the back of Emily's neck.

The frightening pitch and volume let her know Lily was not far off; it sounded as if it came from the direction of the old Bishop's house.

Lily groaned; her lashes fluttered, but she couldn't seem to muster up the energy to open her eyes. Metal hitting hard-packed soil and rocks formed a constant rhythm in her head. Was someone digging?

She pulled in a breath, but something bound her mouth. She tried to move, but her wrists were tightly bound. At her back was a hard surface; she felt with her fingers. It was barn wood, but whose barn?

Lily forced her eyes open; a few feet away from her, the old man from the bridge was busy digging a large hole.

Emily ran toward the field that separated the two properties, her breath hitching and tears spilling from her eyes; she had no idea what the old man was capable of, but if his son was any indication, Lily was in danger!

Emily spotted the Bishop with Lily; she was struggling in his arms, a gag in her mouth and her hands were bound with twine. Her breath hitched, and she bit back tears, wondering how she was going to help her child.

Lord, help me save her!

Emily froze, fear overwhelming her as she watched him carry Lily over to what looked like a freshly-dug grave; the shovel was spade-down in a mound of dirt to the other side of the large hole. That shovel was between them. If he was distracted enough, she could try for it. The spade would make a threatening weapon.

She peered around the corner of the barn, her eyes darting between Lily, who was screaming and kicking, to the shovel she needed to save her.

A twig snapped under her foot and caused the Bishop to whip his head around toward her.

"Who are you?" he barked at her through gritted teeth.

"I am her *mudder!*"

He chuckled. *"Nee,* I remember you! You're Eva's *schweschder*; I made sure that horse tossed her off the bridge, and now you're next," he said, glancing back and forth between her and Lily.

"Eva didn't…" Emily stopped midsentence when she noticed the look of horror on Lily's face. He *had* been there that day, and it was somehow his fault Melody was dead. He'd obviously mistaken her for Eva since they look so much alike.

She gulped; that could have been her if she and Eva were identical twins!

"After I take care of this little witness, I'll take care of you too. I'm not giving you the chance to put me back in jail!"

Lily wriggled in the Bishop's arms. "Help me, *Mamm,*" she cried.

It was the first time she'd recognized Emily as her mother; she would save her daughter, or she would die trying.

"Let her go!" Emily demanded.

She dove for the shovel and grabbed it, rolling onto her side and scrambling to her feet before he could grab her. She raised the shovel over her shoulder. "Don't make me hit you, old man!"

He dropped Lily into the shallow grave and dove for Emily. Lily hit the ground with a groan and then began to cry.

"Help me!" she screamed.

The Bishop tackled Emily and he pinned her down with one arm and raised the shovel above his head with the other.

"Drop it!" a male voice said from behind her. "Drop the shovel and put your hands high where I can see them."

Bishop Byler lowered the shovel slowly, his focus on whoever was facing him. He rose from the ground, and that's when Emily noticed his ankle bracelet blinking nonstop red. She turned around and scooted back toward the officer. They must have come because of the signal.

Lily poked her head up from the shallow grave he'd dug to bury her in; it sent shivers down Emily's spine. She scrambled to her feet as the officers put the Bishop in handcuffs.

She went to Lily and scooped her up into her arms and held her close, allowing her to sob freely.

"It's all over, honey," she said, soothing her daughter. "You're safe now; I'm not going to let anyone hurt you. I love you, Lily."

She laid her head on Emily's shoulder and sniffled. "I love you too, *Mamm.*"

Emily bit back tears of joy; her little girl was safe.

One of the officers approached her. "Are either of you hurt?" he asked.

Emily shook her head. "Just a little scared."

He put a hand on Lily's back and patted her. "There's no reason to be afraid anymore; he'll be going back to jail for a long time."

"How did you know we were here?" she asked.

"We didn't; his alarm tripped several times and then it stayed on because he was out of his zone too long, so we came out here to see why, and that's when we saw him trying to hurt you. Is that a grave he dug?"

Lily lifted her head from Emily's shoulder. "*Jah*, he said he was going to bury me!" she cried. "He's the man who killed my *mudder!*"

Emily fought tears, thinking how close she came to losing Lily.

The officer took their names and address, and then informed them they would be contacted to give a formal statement.

"Would you like a ride home?" the officer asked.

She shook her head. "No, we have something to get, so we'll go back through the field; it isn't far."

"I think I'd feel better if one of us escorted you home," he said.

She nodded; maybe it would be best.

"If we go through the field, it only takes five minutes, but if you go out on the road, it will take longer," she said.

He held a hand out toward the open field. "Lead the way."

Emily and Lily wandered back through the field, hand-in-hand, Emily feeling relieved they were out of danger, and thankful that the police had gotten there in time. But most of all, she felt blessed that Lily had finally accepted her as her mother.

When they came upon the blueberry patch, Emily spotted Lily's full bucket of berries still sitting on the ground and bent to pick it up.

"Let's go home and make some blueberry tarts for your *vadder*, shall we?" she asked.

Lily looked up at her and smiled. "Okay, *Mamm.*

Chapter Fifteen

Emily sat across from Lily at the little table inside the entrance to the garden, sipping meadow tea and nibbling on blueberry tarts.

Lily had talked non-stop about how excited she was for school to begin the following week, but Emily savored every little giggle from her. Sam walked by and smiled at them as he walked the team of draft horses out of the barn so he could bring them to the field to finish the hay-mowing. She watched her husband for a moment, thinking how lucky she was that a man such as Sam loved her.

He'd moved his things back into the main house, and he'd asked her to join him, leaving her childhood bedroom behind. He'd commented the empty room would make a nice place to put Lily's old crib for a new *boppli*, and she'd giggled shyly.

"*Daed*, come sit with us and share our blueberry tarts," Lily begged.

He smiled and tied the horses to the large oak tree in the yard.

"I'd much rather sit and have tea and tarts with *mei familye,*" he said with a chuckle as he sat down between them. "The hay-mowing can wait another day!"

THE END

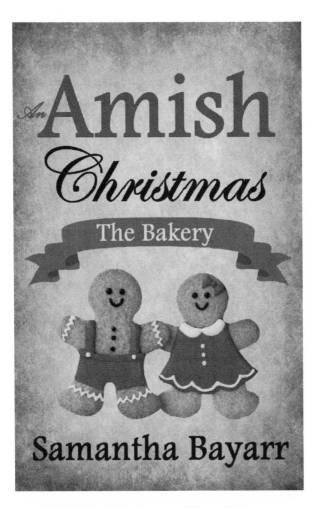

An Amish Christmas

Christmas

The Bakery

Samantha Bayarr

Amish Christmas: The Bakery

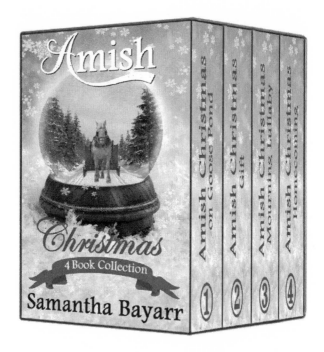

Amish Christmas on Goose Pond — ①
Amish Christmas Gift — ②
Amish Christmas Mourning Lullaby — ③
Amish Christmas Homecoming — ④

Amish
Christmas
4 Book Collection
Samantha Bayarr

Amish Christmas Collection #2

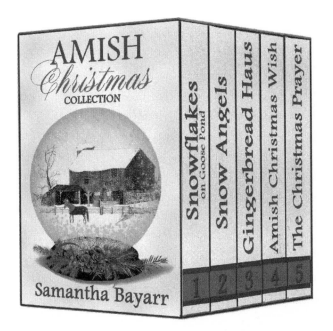

Amish Christmas Collection #1

Newly Released books
always FREE with
Kindle Unlimited.
♡ LOVE to Read?
♡ LOVE Discount Books?
♡ LOVE GIVEAWAYS?

SIGN UP NOW
Click the Link Below to Join
my Exclusive Mailing List

PLEASE CLICK <u>HERE</u> to SIGN UP!

Made in the USA
Columbia, SC
30 March 2018